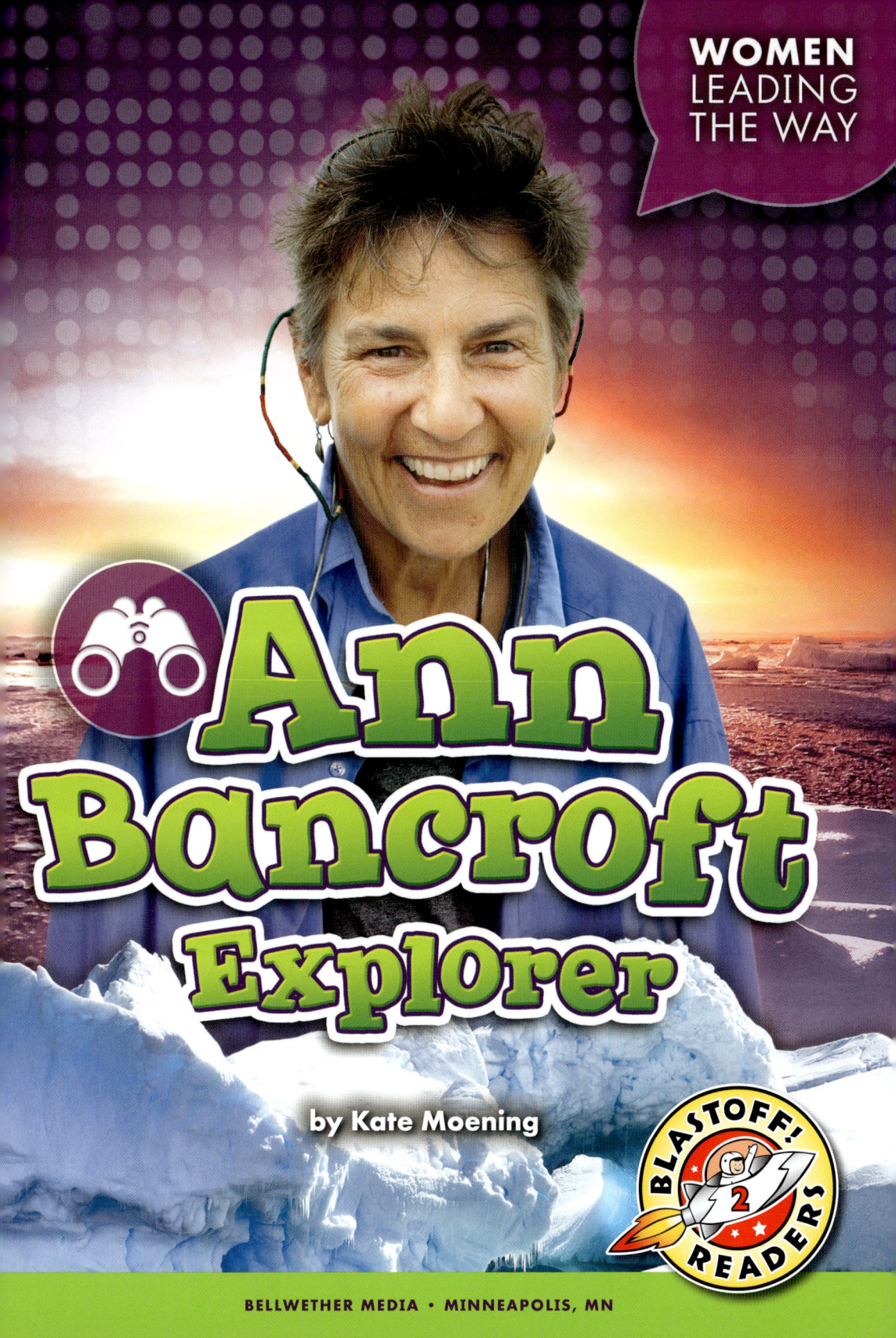

Note to Librarians, Teachers, and Parents:

Blastoff! Readers are carefully developed by literacy experts and combine standards-based content with developmentally appropriate text.

Level 1 provides the most support through repetition of high-frequency words, light text, predictable sentence patterns, and strong visual support.

Level 2 offers early readers a bit more challenge through varied simple sentences, increased text load, and less repetition of high-frequency words.

Level 3 advances early-fluent readers toward fluency through increased text and concept load, less reliance on visuals, longer sentences, and more literary language.

Level 4 builds reading stamina by providing more text per page, increased use of punctuation, greater variation in sentence patterns, and increasingly challenging vocabulary.

Level 5 encourages children to move from "learning to read" to "reading to learn" by providing even more text, varied writing styles, and less familiar topics.

Whichever book is right for your reader, Blastoff! Readers are the perfect books to build confidence and encourage a love of reading that will last a lifetime!

This edition first published in 2020 by Bellwether Media, Inc.

No part of this publication may be reproduced in whole or in part without written permission of the publisher. For information regarding permission, write to Bellwether Media, Inc., Attention: Permissions Department, 6012 Blue Circle Drive, Minnetonka, MN 55343.

Library of Congress Cataloging-in-Publication Data

Names: Moening, Kate, author.
Title: Ann Bancroft : Explorer / by Kate Moening.
Other titles: Blastoff! readers. 2, Women leading the way
Description: Minneapolis, Minnesota : Bellwether Media, Inc., 2020. | Series: Blastoff! readers. Level 2 : Women leading the way | includes index. | Audience: Ages: 5-8. | Audience: Grades: K-1.
Identifiers: LCCN 2019024616 (print) | ISBN 9781644871195 (library binding) | ISBN 9781618917959 (pbk.) | ISBN 9781618917751 (ebook)
Subjects: LCSH: Bancroft, Ann–Travel–Juvenile literature. | Women adventurers–Travel–Arctic regions–Juvenile literature. | Arctic regions–Description and travel–Juvenile literature. | North Pole–Juvenile literature. | Antarctica–Juvenile literature.
Classification: LCC G635.B26 M64 2020 (print) | LCC G635.B26 (ebook) | DDC 910.9163/2–dc23
LC record available at https://lccn.loc.gov/2019024616
LC ebook record available at https://lccn.loc.gov/2019024617

Text copyright © 2020 by Bellwether Media, Inc. BLASTOFF! READERS and associated logos are trademarks and/or registered trademarks of Bellwether Media, Inc.

Editor: Christina Leaf   Designer: Andrea Schneider

Printed in the United States of America, North Mankato, MN.

Table of Contents

Who Is Ann Bancroft?	4
Getting Her Start	6
Changing the World	12
Ann's Future	18
Glossary	22
To Learn More	23
Index	24

Who Is Ann Bancroft?

Ann Bancroft is an **explorer** and a teacher.

She was the first woman to cross **Arctic** ice to reach the **North Pole**!

North Pole

Getting Her Start

Minnesota woods

School was hard for young Ann. She had **dyslexia**. She was also very shy. Sports helped her make friends.

Ann felt free outdoors! She loved exploring Minnesota's woods.

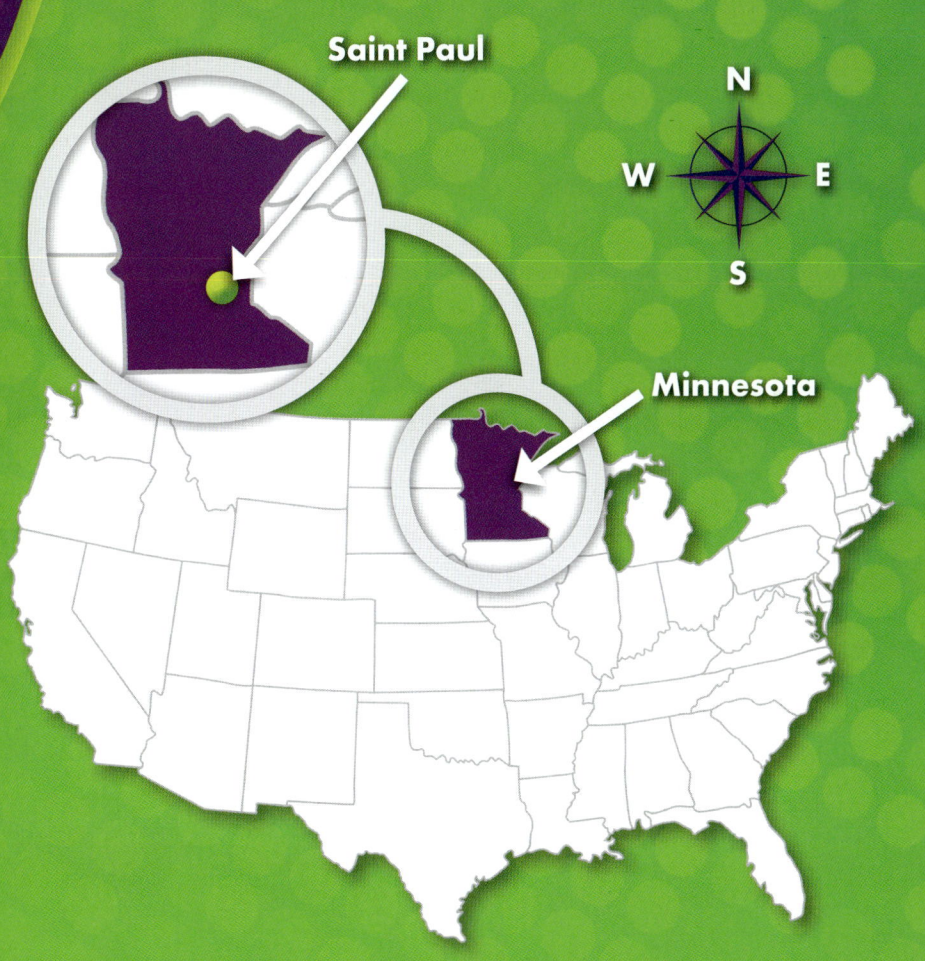

After college, Ann became a teacher. She taught physical education and **special education**.

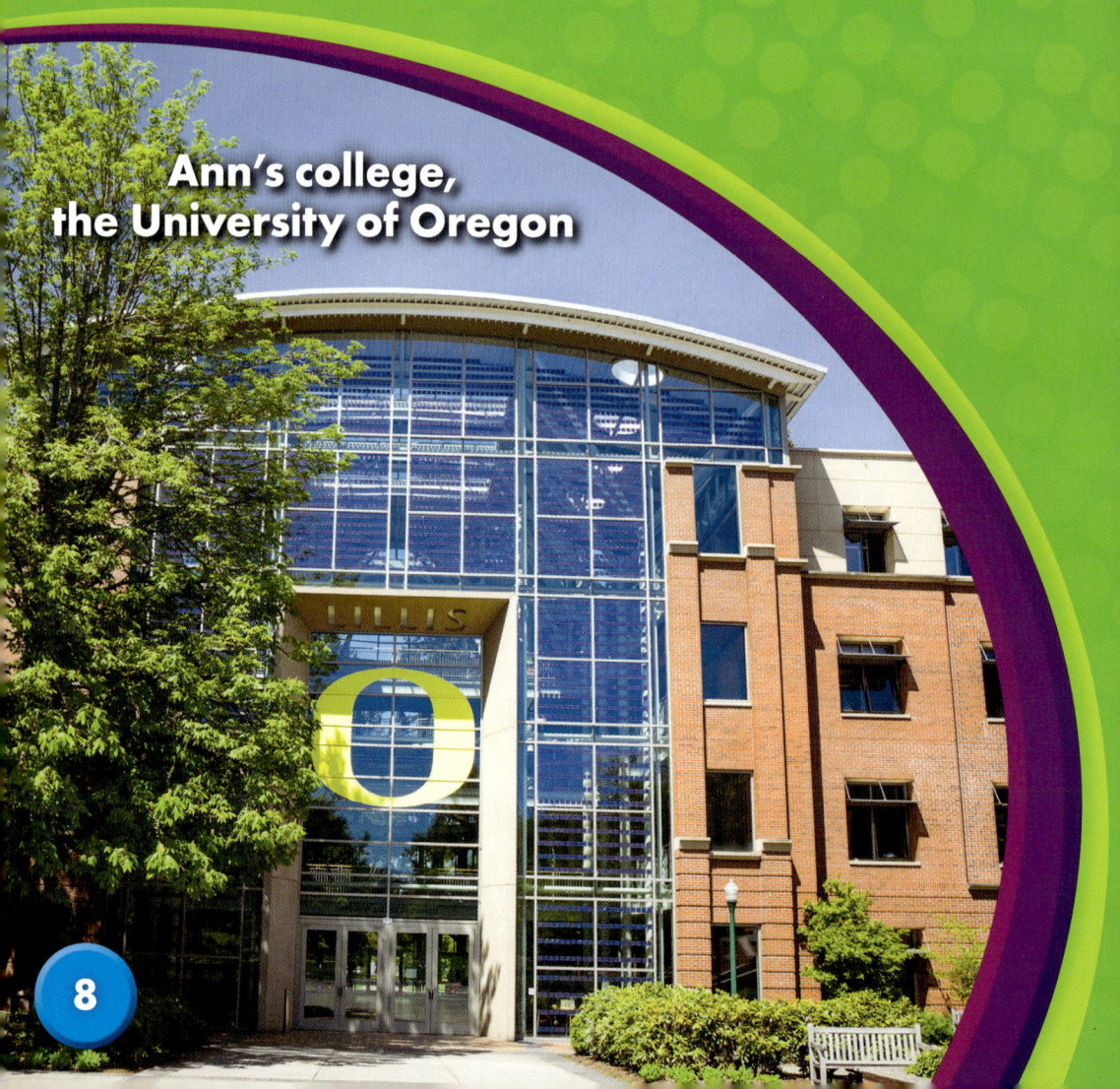

Ann's college, the University of Oregon

Ann Bancroft Profile

Birthday: September 29, 1955
Hometown: Saint Paul, Minnesota
Field: education and polar exploration
Schooling:
- studied physical education

Influences:
- Debbie Bancroft (mother)
- Pat McCart (teacher)

She wanted to help kids who struggled like she did.

In 1986, Ann joined an **expedition** to the North Pole.

She rode with a dogsled team. They crossed 1,000 miles (1,609 kilometers) of Arctic ice!

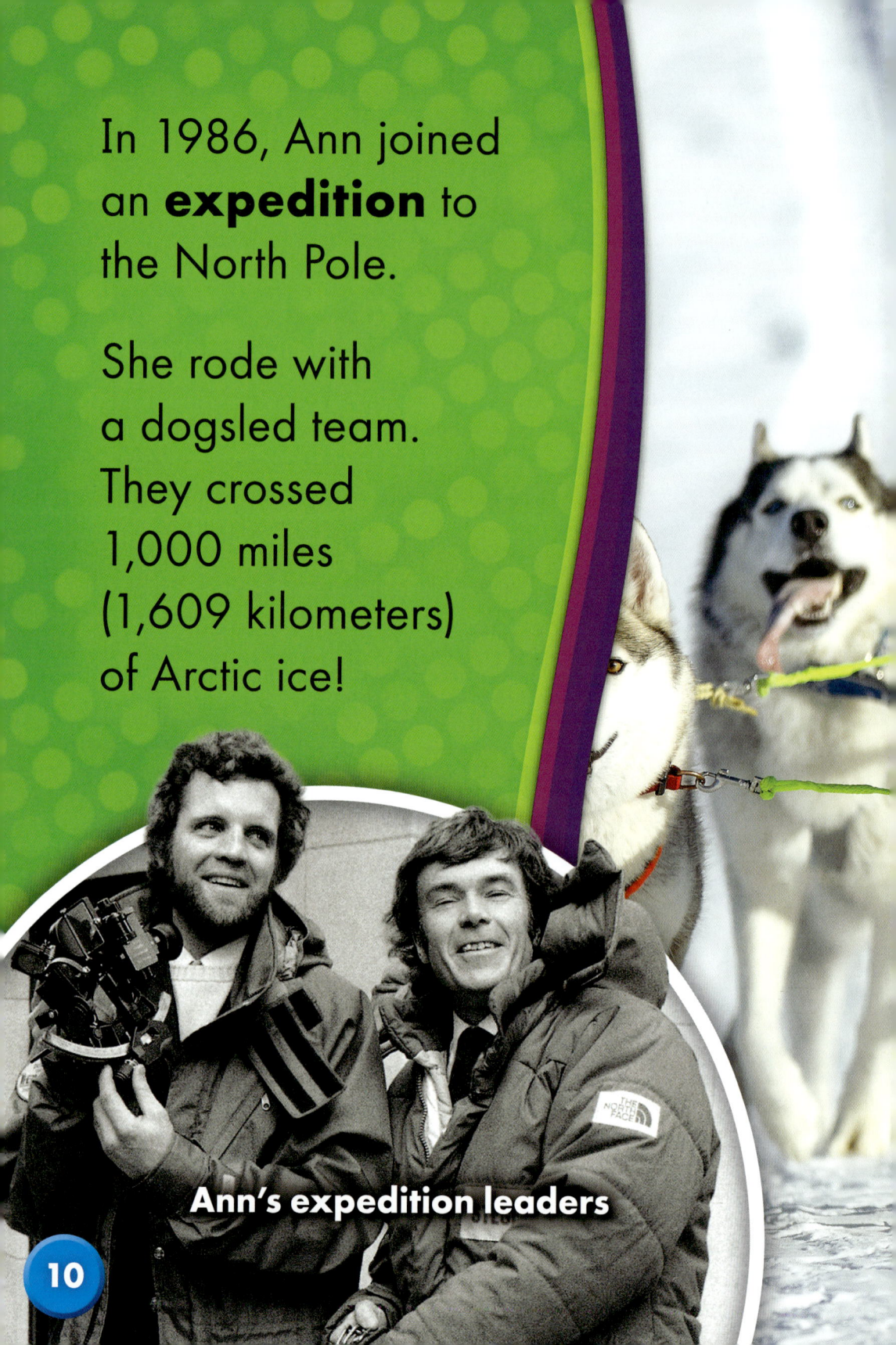

Ann's expedition leaders

dogsled team

Changing the World

Ann and Liv testing equipment

Ann soon led polar expeditions. She and her friend Liv were the first women to ski across Antarctica!

Their adventures **inspired** people everywhere.

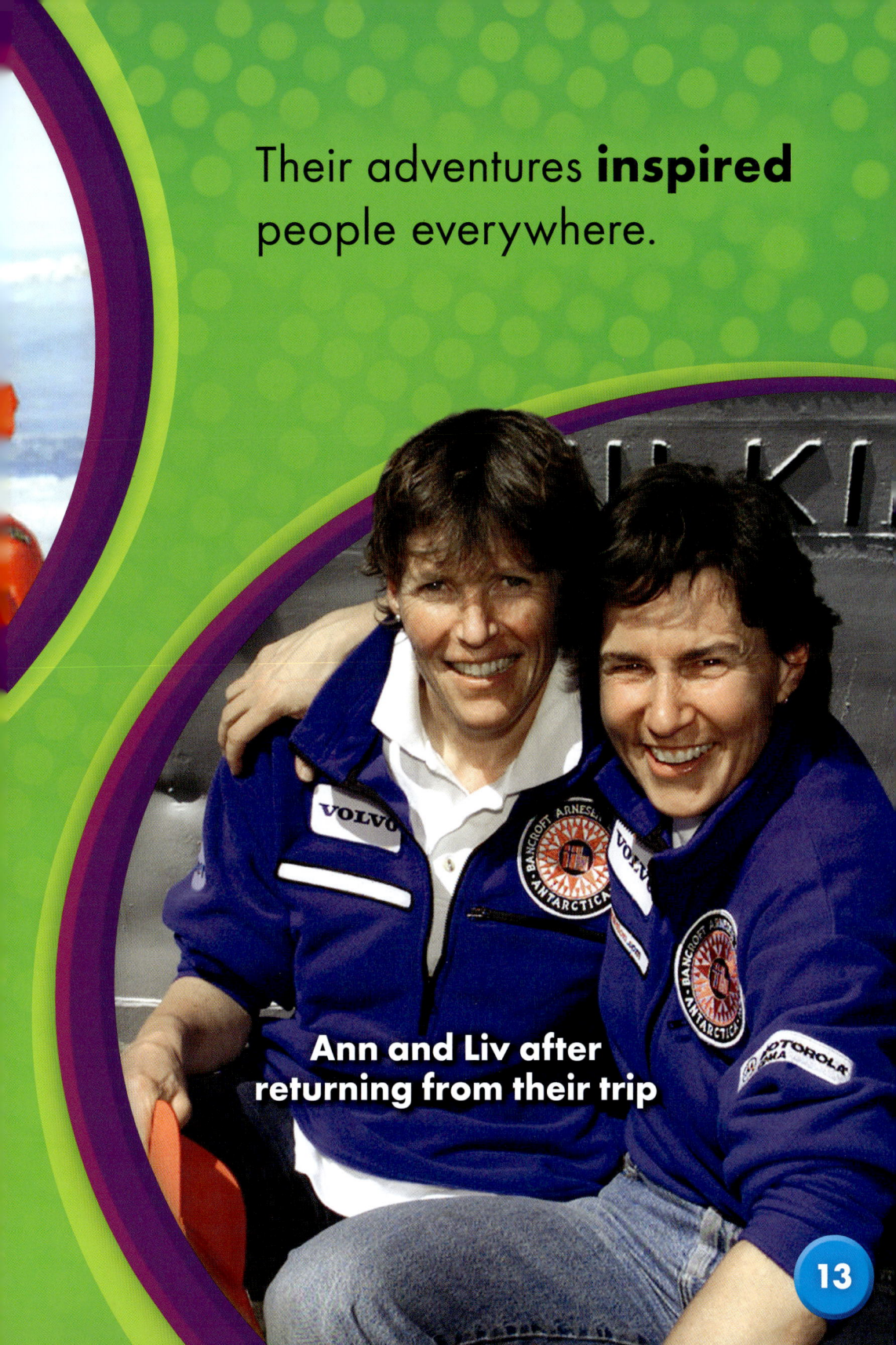

Ann and Liv after returning from their trip

Expeditions were dangerous. Supplies were **limited**.

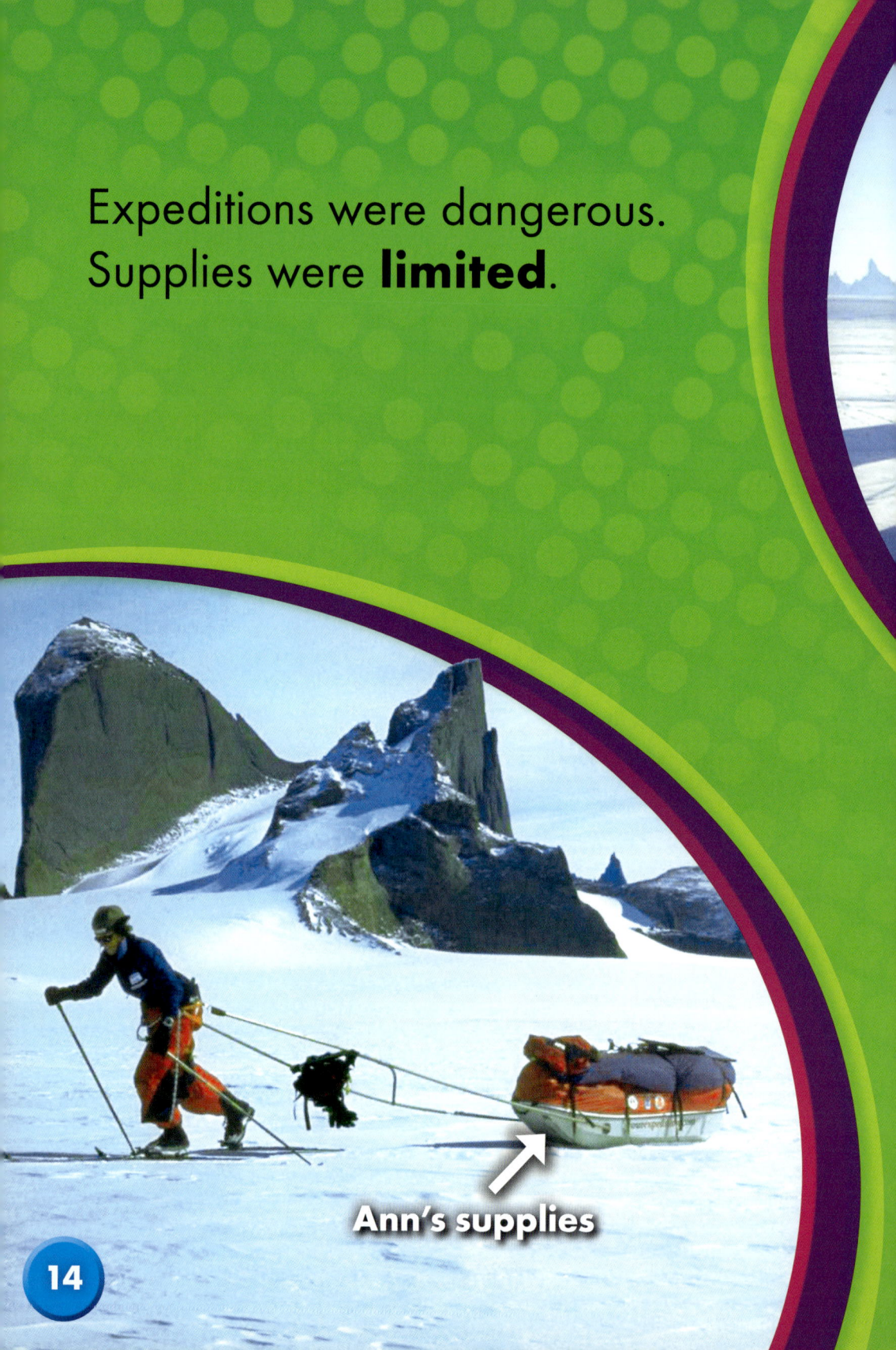

Ann's supplies

Ann and Liv testing their sled in Antarctica

It was also easy to get **frostbite**. The Arctic can reach -70 degrees Fahrenheit (-57 degrees Celsius)!

Ann wanted her experiences to help kids dream big.

She visited schools and talked to students. She started a **foundation** that supports girls and their dreams.

Ann's Future

Today, Ann still has adventures. She and a team are paddling down the world's rivers.

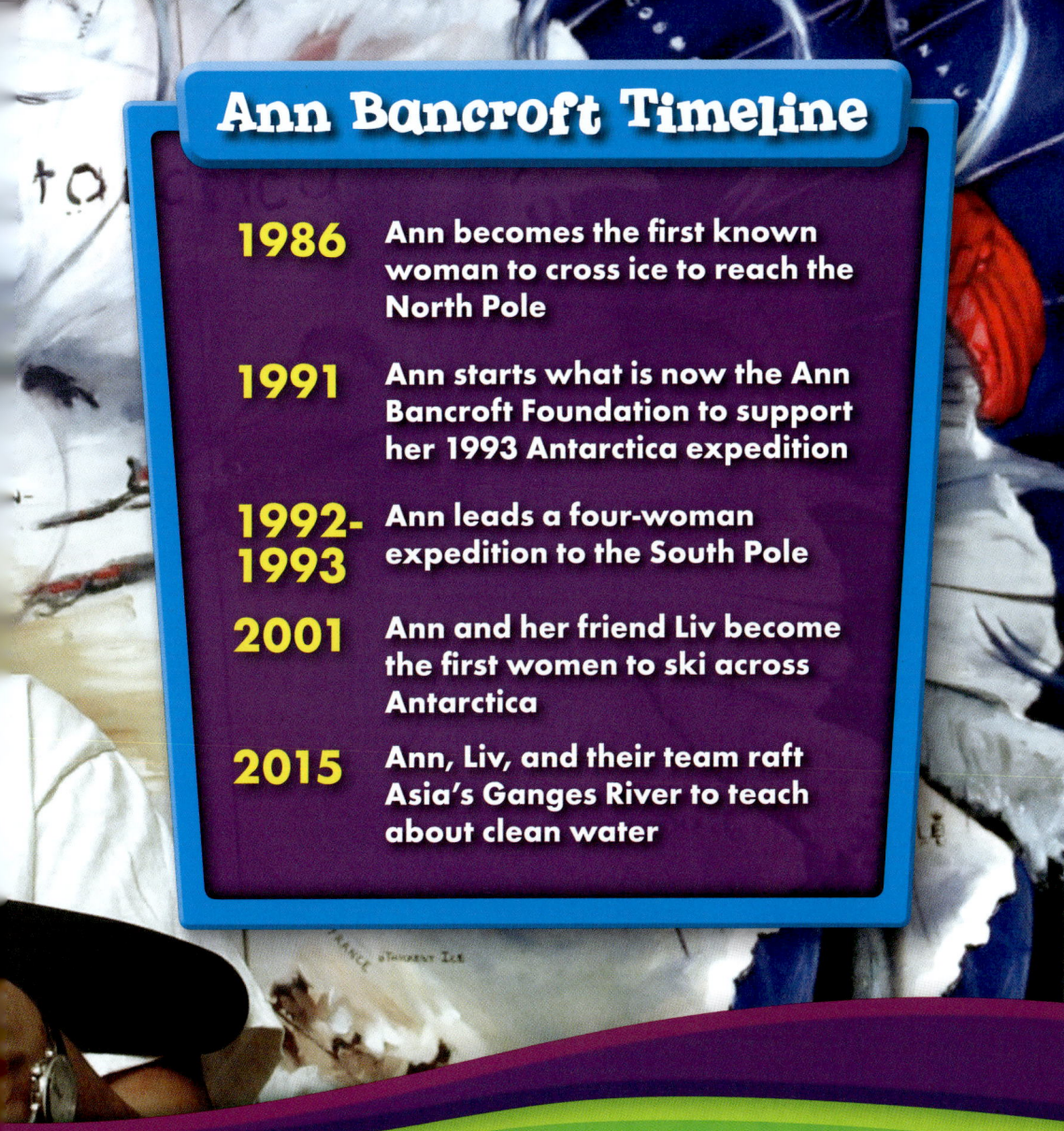

Ann Bancroft Timeline

1986 — Ann becomes the first known woman to cross ice to reach the North Pole

1991 — Ann starts what is now the Ann Bancroft Foundation to support her 1993 Antarctica expedition

1992-1993 — Ann leads a four-woman expedition to the South Pole

2001 — Ann and her friend Liv become the first women to ski across Antarctica

2015 — Ann, Liv, and their team raft Asia's Ganges River to teach about clean water

They want to teach about clean water and **climate change**.

Ann still loves teaching kids outdoors. Her foundation also helps girls find **mentors**.

Ann wants kids to find their own adventures!

Glossary

Arctic—related to the area around the North Pole

climate change—a human-caused process in which Earth's average weather changes over a long period of time

dyslexia—a condition that makes it hard for a person to read, write, and spell words

expedition—a journey by a group of people for a specific purpose, such as research

explorer—a person who travels through a place in order to learn more about it or find something

foundation—a group that gives money in order to do something that helps society

frostbite—an injury that occurs when the skin is exposed to cold for too long

inspired—gave someone an idea about what to do or create

limited—having only a certain amount

mentors—people who teach or give advice

North Pole—the northernmost area of Earth

special education—classes to help students with certain disabilities learn

To Learn More

AT THE LIBRARY
Juarez, Christine. *Antarctica: A 4D Book*. North Mankato, Minn.: Pebble, 2019.

Leaf, Christina. *Rachel Carson: Environmentalist*. Minneapolis, Minn.: Bellwether Media, 2019.

Ryan, Zoë Alderfer. *Ann and Liv Cross Antarctica: A Dream Come True!* Cambridge, Mass.: Da Capo Press, 2001.

ON THE WEB

FACTSURFER

Factsurfer.com gives you a safe, fun way to find more information.

1. Go to www.factsurfer.com.
2. Enter "Ann Bancroft" into the search box and click 🔍.
3. Select your book cover to see a list of related web sites.

Index

adventures, 13, 18, 20
Antarctica, 12, 15
Arctic ice, 4, 10
Arnesen, Liv, 12, 13, 15
climate change, 19
college, 8
dogsled team, 10, 11
dyslexia, 6
expedition, 10, 12, 14
explorer, 4
foundation, 16, 20
frostbite, 15
mentors, 20
Minnesota, 6, 7
North Pole, 4, 10
outdoors, 7, 20
profile, 9
quotes, 5, 17, 21

rivers, 18
school, 6, 16
ski, 12
sports, 6
supplies, 14
teacher, 4, 8, 20
timeline, 19
water, 19

The images in this book are reproduced through the courtesy of: BAE Institute, front cover (Ann), pp. 4-5 (main), 9, 14 (supplies), 20-21 (main); robert mcgillivray, front cover (iceberg); Volodymyr Goinyk, front cover (Arctic background); ppart, pp. 3, 22 (ski equipment); Christopher Meder, p. 4 (inset); JB Manning, pp. 6-7 (woods); Joshua Rainey Photography, p. 8; Marry Lederhandler/ AP Images, p. 10 (inset); Pavel Suhov, pp. 10-11 (main); OBED ZILWA/ AP Images, pp. 12-13 (equipment), 14-15 (sled); Mark Baker/ Reuters/ Newscom, p. 13 (returning), 16-17 (main); Feature Photo Service/ Newscom, p. 16 (inset); Joe Rossi/KRT/ Newscom, pp. 18-19; Photodiem, p. 20 (inset).